A Christmas When the Bells Rang

a

Christmas in the Fandom Book

A Christmas When the Bells Rang

Published by Briny Bindings.

Printed POD by IngramSpark and affiliates, USA.

Author: Tallmadge Swartzfager
Editor: Tallmadge Swartzfager
Layout, Design, Formatting: Tallmadge Swartzfager

ISBN: 979-8-3305-6604-4

A Lamplighter Underground Book

A Christmas When the Bells Rang

a
Christmas in the Fandom Book

Written by:
Tallmadge Swartzfager

Yorkshire,
Northern England

* * *

24th December, 1918

"Last one."

Jack flicked his match into the snow and blew out a great cloud, cigarette pinched between his fingertips. He gazed through the smoke at the surrounding hills and let out a sigh. He looked down at the match as it lay there, already cooled and one end blackened. He stretched out his boot and crushed it into the icy lane for no reason other than to have something to do. He stuck his cigarette in his mouth and clenched his hands, stuffing them deep within his coat pockets, smoking around the cigarette between his lips. He glanced up at his cousin Vibert who was grinning down at him, hanging half-way out the open door of the coach.

"Yeah," he said, "last one."

Vibert swung himself down and walked behind Jack, patting him on the shoulder as he passed. "You shouldn't have started," he said with a wink.

Jack only sighed again. "Daisy would have understood, if she'd known — not that she will."

Jack shot a glance at Vibert, but truth be told neither felt like joking, and Vibert now took his post on the edge of the road, hands in his coat pockets, eyes surveying the snow-blanketed countryside. "Hmm," he grunted in response to Jack, who pulled a hand out and relieved his mouth of the cigarette for a moment before returning both to their proper places.

Snow clung to the trunks of the trees and their branches that overhung the river, flowing full and blood-dark between low and jagged banks of ice. Clouds hung thick and grey above. The Humber had never looked so cold and cruel before.

Vibert remembered another time, when the Humber had flowed clear and mild, the blue sky peaking through the fresh green branches above. He heard the laughter of the ripples slipping over the stones, and then this was joined with other laughter, the laughter of little children he knew, of boys young and strong as yearlings and girls as pretty and sweet as the flowers in their hair. He felt the breeze to his back, gentle and ruffling his hair, not at all biting around his neck and ears and his cheeks and the end of his nose the way the harsh winter winds were wont to as they swept down the Yorkshire moors. He heard running feet behind him, and turning to look was shocked to see Joe bounding across the road, with May and Kate coming through the tall flowers behind him.

They rushed past laughing and shouting, and behind and beside them the snow melted away, and the sun and breeze swept aside all the mud and ice, and suddenly it was spring, spring again! Yet not a new spring, but a spring from long ago.

Joe ran down to the river, and the clear blue sky brushed the clouds slowly off its face. Margery and Frederick were walking along the far bank with Little Robert toddling between them, and as someone called to them with a sing-song voice they looked up and waved, calling back across the river. Away on the hillsides behind them he could see people walking, sitting, chatting — all guests at the wedding, cousins and future in-laws and close friends.

"Vibert!"

He looked down sharply to the river, and saw poking up over the tall grass a familiar, young, beautiful face.

"Vibert!" Polly called again, "come down here!"

She was looking right at him. He turned to see if there was anyone behind him, and then came back around to see Emmie standing there beside Polly, hands on her hips.

"Vibert, you naughty boy, quit playing coy and come down here," his sister chided with a grin.

He looked down at himself, and to his shock the trench coat, uniform trousers, and old, hopelessly faded though stout boots were gone, and he was there in his old shoes that he had not seen in four years, brown slacks and waistcoat — he reached up for his moustache and found only his smooth upper lip. Drat, that had taken him months to produce. Oh well, Polly preferred him clean-shaven anyway.

"Come on!" Emmie waved to him.

Down the grassy slope he loped, lifting his feet high and clapping his hat down lest the wind pull it off his head, a smile breaking over his face. He sprang into the shorter grass around the trees there beside the river and slid to a halt beside Emmie and Polly.

"What kept you, Vibert?" asked Polly, smiling up from the blanket where she sat.

"Well, nothing," Vibert shrugged.

"Vibert was probably afraid to get his shoes dirty, the little fop," teased Emmie, sitting beside her.

"Hadn't occurred to me," Vibert said carelessly, glancing down at his shoes and lifting one of his feet to inspect, "though perhaps as best-man I ought to be more careful."

"His cousin gets married and suddenly he feels pretentious and important," said Emmie to Polly in that same tone of playful mockery.

"My sister gets married and he somehow feels responsible for making sure the day's festivities go off without a hitch," answered she.

"That they get hitched without a hitch," quipped Vibert. Emmie rolled her eyes. "Or that they tie the knot without any tie-ups?"

"Oh, do go on, Vibert," said Emmie, raising herself up with Polly sitting between them.

"Over here, Toddles!" Polly called, waving past Vibert to her youngest sister. Vibert turned to see the little girl, closing in on ten, running up the row of old trees who hung their boughs all around the river bank; and there, running behind her, laughing loud and merrily, was Will.

"Vibert, save me!" Toddles cried with a giggle, running to him.

"Vibert?" said he, grabbing her and throwing her into the air — she was just a little slip of a girl — and then catching her and setting her back down on her feet. "I thought Jack was your favourite — or is Daisy not sharing him?"

Toddles, who could not be "Toddles" for much longer, laughed and retreated to Emmie, taking cover from Will's pursuit behind her skirts.

"Will Redfern, what is the meaning of this?"

Will, stopping to pant beside Vibert, looked dumbstruck at the question and thought for a brief moment. "You know, I — I don't know! Toddles, why was I chasing you?"

"I ate a Russian Tea-ball," Toddles whispered up to Emmie, loud enough for everyone to hear.

"Oh, you pesky little wench!" exclaimed Emmie, kneeling down and tickling her, "you're as naughty as Vibert!"

"We learned from the best!" Toddles tried to tickle her back, laughing and wiggling.

"Ah! Saucy girl!" Emmie gasped, laughing along, "who taught you to be rude to your elders?"

Now Emmie had her in her arms and she was in real trouble — there was no escaping these tickles!

"Vibert, help me!"

"No, you've already asked that before — I don't like doing the same thing twice. Besides, Toddles, I'm a very busy man when I'm in the country," he began to gesture to the trees and hills around them, "there are woods to explore, and game to hunt — and lots of pretty young ladies —"

"Mary! Lucy!" May's shout came from the river-bank. "Polly, Emmie! Mary is here!"

"Mary!" exclaimed Toddles, breaking free from Emmie and running back down the river with the others.

"Oh! All the Brandons are here!" Emmie rose to follow and bring the girls — Jack's sister Lucy who had come up yesterday and their cousin Mary who must have just got in — up to their little "picnic". Will ran off too, being at that point of youth where any excuse to run is a good one however utterly pointless it may seem to "grown-ups".

"A simple wedding," chuckled Polly, looking after them, "small, and nothing fancy — but I wouldn't be surprised if all the Butlers were still invited."

"Weren't they?"

"I don't know about Barak and Tamsin's families," Polly hugged her knees, "but …"

The group was all coming back, and Polly rose to greet her kinswomen.

Vibert silently and subtly excused himself from the little moot and retreated to the edge of the lawn where the moor became meadow-like. Will and Joe soon gravitated towards him, and the three of them stood there experiencing a certain awe at what they saw: a gaggle of girls.

The herd mentalities of men and women are completely and unbridgeably different. Men in a group will become very loud and in some way violent, either looking for something to collectively hunt or more often competing with each other to assert dominance — that is, when men are boys. Women at every stage of development will assemble themselves peacefully and quietly together, by instinct and respect recognize a leader, and soon engage in pleasant and edifying conversation that if left unchecked will result in some sort of party or the formation of a charitable organisation that will soon have the entire county living in much improved conditions.

Thus the boys stood dumbfounded as Emmie, already the matron of this gaggle of girls, led the young ladies in a conversation about the bride-to-be that the three young gentlemen could not understand more than ten words of. This did not last overly long, though, for Toddles was much too interested in playing with them to let the older girls go on and on, and May and Kate too wanted to go back down to the river.

Skipping off and calling out, "Boats, Will! Come on, Joe!" they led everyone down to the river.

So they sent little paper boats down the river to find the sea beyond Hull, rollicked and frolicked along the banks, and ran chasing each other through the flowers on the moor in so many children's games and romps. It seemed to go on forever, that morning, though it was only a few hours — short, precious hours they would look back upon some day, in the spring of 1914. Lunch would come soon, and after that Daisy and Jack were to be married in the little chapel.

They were so happy, Jack and Daisy — and he was so handsome and strong, and she so beautiful and young. The whole world was before them, and what made it better is that they would share it, wherever they went and whatever they did.

Emmie, Lucy, and Mary were walking down the river bank discussing something relating to the day. May, Kate, and Toddles were sitting amidst the flowers, making themselves dairy-chains and crowns. Will and Joe were doing their best to catch fish — shoes, socks, and jackets on the bank, pants-legs and shirt-sleeves rolled up, laughing and gigging away with pointed sticks they had hastily carved with pen-knives, moving rocks to build dams and trying to corner their quarry.

Will had his cap on jauntily, and that was the only weight in the world he carried. His blonde hair made him look like part of the world of grass and brush that was the moors, and he laughed like a gust of wind and moved like the breeze through the heath. Joe, with his dark hair, belonged to the river, to the cool water and the shade of the trees, laughing like ripples sliding over stones, his movements slower and smoother than his brother's.

Vibert was standing leaning against one of the trees, Polly sitting among the roots beside him, watching the river slip by them — and the fish slip by her brothers.

"I remember the day Jack first came to visit," said Polly, "Toddles never left Daisy's side, she just clung to her arm and stared at Jack, not sure what to do with him but knowing that he was there to take her sister away — but he grew on her."

"Explains why she got accustomed to me so quickly."

"Have you come to take her sister away?"

Vibert glanced down. Polly was smiling up at him with that smile she had.

"Because if you have," she said, frowning suddenly and looking away at the river, "you'd better give up those pretty young women you were talking about earlier."

Vibert was confused in several ways, and blinking profusely stammered out, "Who?"

"All those pretty young ladies you were telling Toddles about earlier."

"Oh, them! Ha-ha —"

"Them?" Polly looked up at him sharply.

"No! Not *them* - there is no *them*, Polly, I —"

Polly started laughing. "You are too easy, Vibert! Emmie was right: you are gullible!"

Vibert laughed too. Then he squatted down next to her and looked her straight in her eyes. She smiled again and everything Vibert had been ready to say tripped over itself and scattered away in a million tiny pieces.

"Polly …" He could barely bring his voice above a whisper suddenly.

"Yes, Vibert?" Polly whispered back.

"Polly —" Vibert chuckled at how involuntarily silly he had become, and Polly giggled too. "Polly, my nymph, I know Christmas was not all that long ago, and I still have not decided what I am going to do with my life and am therefore far from being established as Jack is, but Polly if you'll promise to marry me … well, I'd be very happy and I'll always try to make you happy, and keep you safe when the time comes."

Sunlight reflecting off the water danced across her face, and the breeze brushed her hair across her young, flushed cheeks.

"Yes, Vibert," she said softly, eyes shining and lips toying with another smile, "I promise to marry you — someday."

"No later than is absolutely necessary," said Vibert, grasping her hand in both of his. He caught himself and released it, but she pressed hers back into his, and covered them with her other.

"As soon as we can," she said, leaning closer to him.

"Practically speaking," added Vibert, taking both her hands in his and rubbing her small knuckles with his thumbs, looking down at them the whole while, "of course."

Polly stifled a laugh. "Of course. When did you start becoming so practical and … dull — like Bruce?"

Vibert laughed. "I beg your pardon!"

"Vibert! Polly! Boys! Come on, we have to get started!"

"Coming, Emmie!"

Vibert leapt up and helped Polly to her feet. They stood there for a moment, hands in hands, staring at each other. Polly smiled. The phrase "Redfern vixen" suggested itself to his mind.

"Polly," he began, then added quickly, "I'll kiss you later," before taking off after Will and Joe. "I'm right behind you, Will! Go, hurry!"

"Something to look forward to," said Polly, watching him go. Then suddenly she turned and looked up the snow-blanketed slope directly into Vibert's eyes.

"That's it."

The vision of that spring four years ago vanished entirely and Vibert looked over at Jack. He was straightening his up-turned collar, cigarette butt sending up its last puff of smoke from the snow.

"What was that?"

"That's it," repeated Jack, "the end of the last cigarette."

"Ah," Vibert rubbed a hand across his forehead.

He had almost forgotten — those lines he and his wife wrote at the end of each letter, that they had said to each other the day he left for France — they had started that here, beside the Humber, one day in spring, when they were all younger. How soon it had all changed, and it felt like so long ago — how different it all was, the river frozen, Will gone, and no one young anymore. Not really.

"Come on, Vibert," Jack said, foot on the step, ready to pull himself back up into the coach, "they'll be waiting for us."

The coach, mounted on runners for the snow, was incredibly smooth. It had an interesting effect on the cousins and brothers-in-law: accustomed to bumpy rides and rough accommodations, it was too unnatural for them to be truly comfortable.

"Bruce and Helen ought to be there when we arrive — blastedly inconvenient, the paperwork for letting Myst Hall and all. But Bruce knows what he's doing, and I'm sure he squared everything with the renters in a jiff."

"Rather — and Joe has certainly beaten us home. Lucky tar. Who's renting the estate there?"

"An American family, Fitz-something or other. Emmie said they are a good family, kind people. The father is some sort of lawyer."

They glided along in silence for a while.

"I always have wanted to spend Christmas in Yorkshire," said Vibert.

"Well, Happy Christmas, cousin."

Outside the coach the countryside slid by in a sea of white and grey, the snow only broken by the shadow-like forms of the proud stones that stood in their ancient watch over the heaths and moors. Stone fences, like black and grey snakes frozen still and thinly blanketed in snow, wound and criss-crossed across the landscape, while within their coils the native sheep, looking like animate beasts of rock and snow, stood about nuzzling and nibbling on hay supplied them.

These lifted their heads carelessly as the coach glided by, watching apathetically the homeward trek of two young men lately returned from war. It caused Vibert to think of Odysseus and the sheep of Zeus — and he thanked the living God for bringing him and his cousin safely home.

The sides of the road were banded like the sheep fields with these stone walls, and where these were absent they gave way to low dikes where tufts of dry, brown grass stuck up from the snow, interspersed with small, gnarled trees, scions of those lonely sentinels who stood upon the ridge lines, spreading their branches in every direction, reaching towards the ancient memory of the vast forests that had once covered all this island realm — a memory whose history was written only in the soil and stones of these lands.

The grey sky above hardly stood in contrast to the endless monotony of the world beneath it, except that the proud hills, those last epitaphs to mountains filled with monsters and dragons that had stood in the days of kings forgotten who had slept long before the advent of King Arthur, struck like defiant fists their heads up against the horizon. But even this was no sharp or sudden — the hills, old as the earth, were squat things, without any truly jagged edges — blunt knives thrashing weakly against the veiled sky, a feeble protest against the cold and the growing dark.

They rode over hills and bridges until as twilight covered the world in purple shadows they came within sight of the town. Suddenly the church bells began to ring. Vibert looked out the window and cocked a brow at Jack. Jack smiled. The coach slid to a stop in front of a large house of wood and stone. They hopped out, and their feet had barely reached the ground before they were surrounded by their family, being hugged and kissed and cried on and cheered over.

"Jack! Jack! You're back!"

"Toddles! My, how you're grown!"

Bruce, Mr Trevor, and Mr Redfern pulled the boy's luggage down from the coach. Daisy pressed a little boy into Jack's arms, and he held his son for the first time. Joe suddenly came running up, quite out of breath.

"They said to ring the bells for you, Jack!" he gasped, smiling broadly.

"To welcome you safely home," Daisy kissed him.

They all went inside, Joe playing a song on the fiddle, Bruce and Helen acting as host and hostess to the whole family. Peels of laughter, the first and heartiest the house had heard in a long time, rang out across the snow with the bells, and at last there was peace on earth. God was in heaven, and in their hearts, and it was Christmas once more.

O Christmas, happy Christmas!
Is it really come again,
With its memories and greetings,
With its joy and with its pain?
There's a minor in the carol,
And a shadow in the light,
And a spray of cypress twining
With the holly wreath to-night.
And the hush is never broken
By laughter light and low,
As we listen in the starlight
To the "bells across the snow."

O Christmas, happy Christmas!
'Tis not so very long
Since other voices blended
With the carol and the song!
If we could but hear them singing
As they are singing now,
If we could but see the radiance
Of the crown on each dear brow;
There would be no sigh to smother,
No hidden tear to flow,
As we listen in the starlight
To the "bells across the snow."

O Christmas, happy Christmas!
This never more can be;
We cannot bring again the days
Of our unshadowed glee.
But Christmas, happy Christmas,
Sweet herald of good-will,
With holy songs of glory
Brings holy gladness still.
For peace and hope may brighten,
And patient love may glow,
As we listen in the starlight
To the "bells across the snow."

O Christmas, happy Christmas!
Is it really come again,
With its memories but fleeting,
Of our sorrow and our pain?
For there's a song on the wind,
In the shadow shines a light,
And down in lowly Bethlehem
A babe was born to-night.
And the curse of sin is broken:
The Kingdom's seeds will grow!
As we listen in the starlight
To the "bells across the snow."

Look out for these Releases From the "Christmas in the Fandom" Series!!!

Christmas at Myst Hall (1913)
Publication Date TBD

A Christmas Far From Home (1914)
Released May of 2024!

A Christmas Dark and Cold (1915)
Publication Date TBD

Christmas for Willy Redfern (1916)
Released Christmas of 2024!

Keep the Home Fires Burning (1917)
Publication Date TBD

A Christmas When the Bells Rang (1918)
Released Christmas of 2024!

www.ingramcontent.com/pod-product-compliance
Lightning Source LLC
Chambersburg PA
CBHW051251150726
48001CB00019B/2560

* 9 7 9 8 3 3 0 5 6 6 0 4 4 *